Camp Prodigy

STAIRS

Camp Prodigy

Caroline Palmer

ATHENEUM BOOKS FOR YOUNG READERS
New York London Toronto Sydney New Delhi

ATHENEUM BOOKS FOR YOUNG READERS

An imprint of Simon & Schuster Children's Publishing Division

1230 Avenue of the Americas, New York, New York 10020

The text for this book was set in CarolinePalmer.
The illustrations for this book were digitally rendered.

Manufactured in China
0224 SCP
First Edition
2 4 6 8 10 9 7 5 3 1

Library of Congress Cataloging-in-Publication Data
Names: Palmer, Caroline (Comics creator), author, artist.
Title: Camp prodigy / Caroline Palmer.
Description: First Atheneum Books for Young Readers hardcover edition. | New York : Atheneum Books for Young Readers, 2024. | Audience: Ages 8-12 | Summary: "A heartwarming middle grade graphic novel following two nonbinary kids who navigate anxiety and identity all while having fun and forming friendships at their summer orchestra camp"- Provided by publisher.
Identifiers: LCCN 2023042106 (print) | LCCN 2023042107 (ebook) | ISBN 9781665930383 (hardcover) | ISBN 9781665930376 (trade paperback) | ISBN 9781665930390 (ebook)
Subjects: CYAC: Graphic novels. | Anxiety-Fiction. | Gender identity-Fiction. | Friendship-Fiction. | Camps-Fiction. | LCGFT: Graphic novels.
Classification: LCC PZ7.7.P1646 Cam 2024 (print) | LCC PZ7.7.P1646 (ebook) | DDC 741.5/973-dc23/eng/20231114
LC record available at https://lccn.loc.gov/2023042106
LC ebook record available at https://lccn.loc.gov/2023042107

For the kids under pressure.
Don't be so hard on yourself;
there's always someone
out there who can help.

Eli
Viole
At the young age o
Violet is an acclai
iolist. They bega
er playing in t
aria Youth Orch
and this is their fi
tour.
Violet identifies as
nonbinary, neither
nor female. They are

Oh!

OVERTURE

March
EMPLOYEE ONLY
This isn't the bathroom.

I have ten minutes until the concert...

The Inspiration Concerto

Oh! I just wanted to...
STAFF
...find the bathroom.
Yup, you're definitely lost!
STAFF
You're gonna
ve to take
right
at the...

You sound beautiful, baby!
Mom!
Thanks.
How're you feeling, Eli? You seem nervous.
I-
The concert's about to start! We're gonna need you onstage, Mx. Violet.

–am feeling great!
See ya soon.
And don't worry. I got this all down perfectly...
There you are, Tate!
Sorry, I couldn't find the bathroom.
Yeesh, embarrassing...
Blah blah blah.
Now, it's my pleasure to introduce...
...the renowned child prodigy Eli Violet!

Don't screw up.
Don't screw up.
Don't screw up.
Gotta be perfect.
No mistakes.
like that
Mx. Violet?

Nope.

We...are very sorry, everyone.

It seems Mx. Violet is unable to perform today, due to a... family emergency.

In their stead, please enjoy the Substitute Symphony, as played by our orchestra.

You may contact us about compensation after the show.

mumble

mumble

mumble

mumble

mumble

Oh, man! I wonder what happened...
Hmm.
mumble
mumble
mumble
Weird.
...
Okay... you look **super** bummed about this for some reason.
What? No, I just...
I don't know why, but it felt like...
...we were about to hear something really special.

I. FANTASI

June

wik
wok

waaahh

Pbbth

The "THIS STINKS" ADAGIO

I think I'm getting *worse*.

Tate! Dinnertime!

Coming!

I heard you practicing upstairs. It sounds good, kiddo!
Mm. Thanks.
glance
You've really been improving since you joined the school orchestra.
I can't wait for your concert next week!
Yeeeeep! It's gonna be really...awesome!
And you're sure you're ready for this? You've only been playing viola for a few months.
If you need a bit more time to–

No, no, don't worry! I'm doing fine. I'm great!
I'm ready for the concert, it's gonna be great, and everything's just really...
...great.
catch!
Uh.
I hit a double today at baseball practice.
HI-5
Awesome, Ian!
Pchooo.
phew
Maybe *you* should think about doing a sport next year, too, Tate!
Hmm!

It'll help you grow up into a nice...
... young...
MAN...
Sorry, I'm full.
Mm.
Thanks for dinner, Dad.

It was great.

Sigh
FWUMP

...

Nat

Can I tell you something important

e you would not
ELIEVE wat just
ppened to me :((
Can I tell you something important

can i vent to you? bc this is soooooo annoying

Q W E R T Y U I O P
A S D F G H J K
Z X C V B N M
tap tap tap

Im listening!

I don't get it...
Am I not good enough to play in the concert?
It's not a matter of skill, Tate.
You know I want you to succeed in this class.
But success is not constantly pushing yourself to your limits.
It's clear you've been frustrated this quarter, and I understand.
There are a lot of students in this class, and it's difficult to give everyone enough individual attention.
Despite that, you've been improving very quickly. It's impressive!
But it's okay to take breaks when you need them.
And if you *do* decide to sit this concert out, you won't be the only one. Not by a long shot.

Refusing to rest when you're frustrated won't help you improve.
It's like art block! You have to step away and do other things so you can relax and regain your inspiration.
Do you understand what I'm trying to tell you, Tate?
...Yeah.
I'll sit out of the concert this year.
BRIIIIING...
chatter chatter

Hey, dude, scoot over!

Sure.

DUDE

So, how was your day?

Ehhh...

Good, because mine *sucked*.

Ian?
Hey, Ian?
tap
tap
What?
I kind of...
Cringe...
...need advice.
Hold your horses— Is this really *happening*?
Are you actually gonna tell me about your *feelings*?
Sit down, little bro. The doctor is *in*.
Ugh, just the worst.
Well...

Why don't you say something like...

...

You're sitting out because you want your first concert to be with kids who are a bit more serious about music.

Is that weird?

Is it true?

...

CAMP PRODIGY

To those who are just starting out, there's no need to be intimidated! The camp isn't too intensive, and you can learn from skilled peers.

To those looking for something a little more ...anced, you'll be able to ...n and guide the ...ginners. Likewise, each ...ection has a solo part you can audition for in the end-of-camp concert.

"A place for all musicians, from beginner to advanced!"

Camp Prodigy is a monthlong string orchestra camp for middle schoolers.

Grow as a musician while enjoying fun activities around camp.

Weekly nature hikes, arts and crafts, talent shows, swim days at the lake, and more!

You'll connect with peers who are just as passionate about music as you are.

We know how much you love viola, and-
You're saying...
CAMP PRODIGY
...I could go here?
Of course!
If you want to.

Thank you.

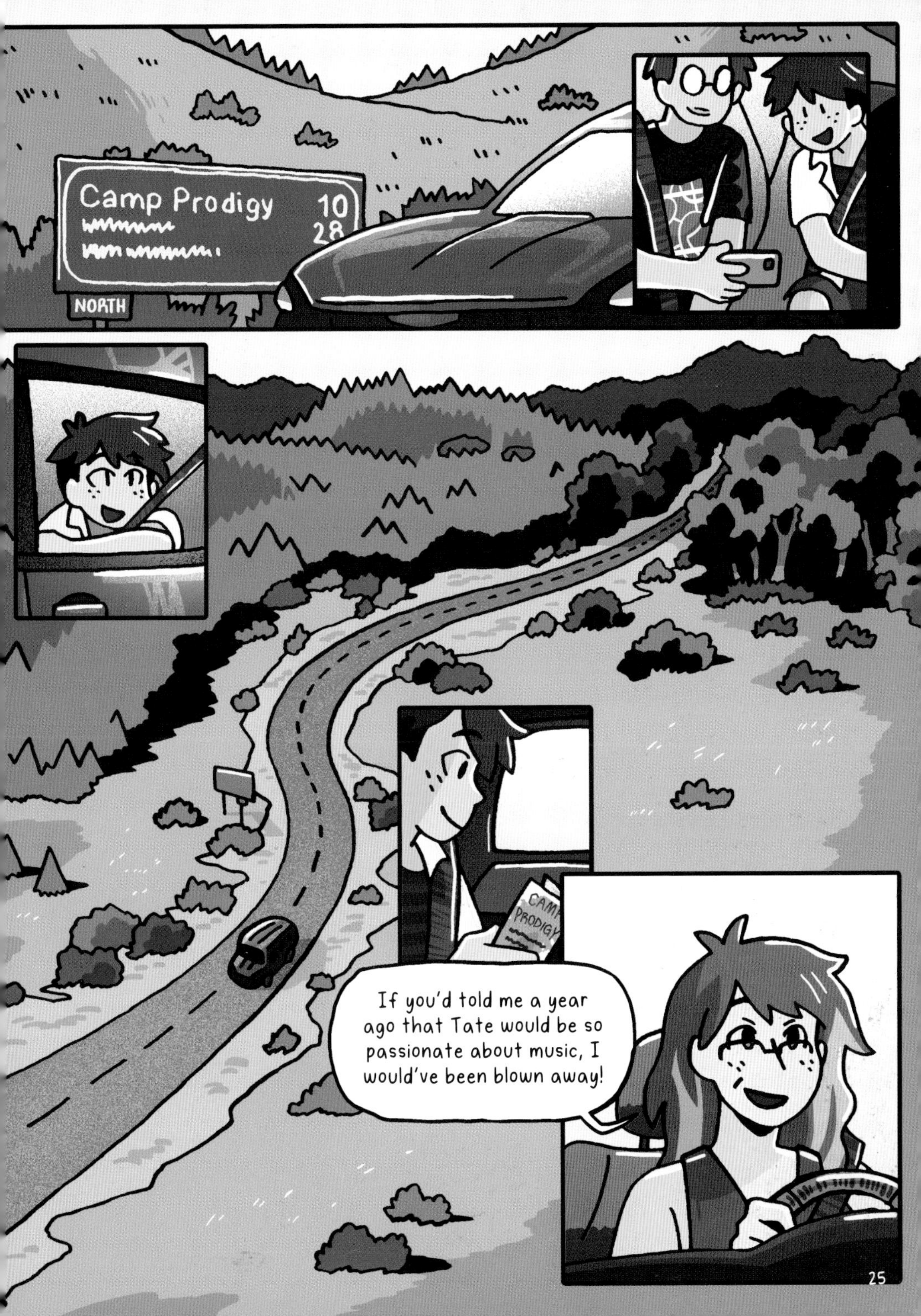
Camp Prodigy 10
28
NORTH
CAMP PRODIGY
If you'd told me a year ago that Tate would be so passionate about music, I would've been blown away!

It certainly came on fast. How did it start, Tate?
Eli Violet's concert!
Really?
Of course! I... Well, I looked them up afterward, and they're amazing!
That was pretty weird, though.
The way the concert was canceled?
Well, yeah. But the orchestra played something nice in the end. I just thought...
Eli Violet. She was weird, wasn't she?

Oh, her! There was a lot of talk about how she is "nonbinary," or something like that.
I've been hearing that word a lot these days, but I don't have a clue what it means!
It just seems a little silly.
Look! I, uh, think we're here!
WELCOME CAMPERS!!

We're dropping off Tate Seong.
Great! Let me just mark him down.
CAMP PRODIGY

These forms are going to take a while, so why don't you get to know some of the other campers?
Tate?

There are about thirty minutes until the opening assembly. You can use that time to socialize!
11:28
Um...
Go ahead, Tate!
If you make friends *now*, you can be socially awkward *later*.

Yeah, okay! I'll go.
Great!
chatter
chatter
chatter
chatter
chatter
chatter
chatter
Uh, hi! What are you doing?

Do you know how to play Euchre?
What's Euchre?
tsk.
GONG.
...
We're trying to get backstage to check out the cool sound equipment.
Wanna come? We could totally Rickroll everyone!
You're a... Taurus.
Am I right?
Casey – cellist
Benji – bassist
Harper – bassist

I'm memorizing everyone's names! Tell me if I get yours wrong, Tart!
Ruby – violinist

?
Seb – cellist

I just grabbed this branch outside because I thought it was neat...
Am I gonna get in trouble?
Peter – violinist

It's...nice to meet you!

11:37

Hi! Nice bracelet.

Thanks!

D'you braid them too?
I used to. It was a fun hobby!
Awesome!!

My name's Maya. I play the viola.

I'm Tate. And same!

Ooh, maybe we'll be bunking in the same cabin!
Maybe!

Hey, do you smell that?
chatter
chatter
Chatter
Chatter
Chatter
GASP! I love breakfast muffins!
You're just handing these out?
My goal is to be concert master, so I'm bribing everyone.
Hannah – violinist
Kidding.
I got nervous about going to an overnight camp for a whole month, so I was stress-baking this morning.

Kidding again.
Or am I?
Hah!

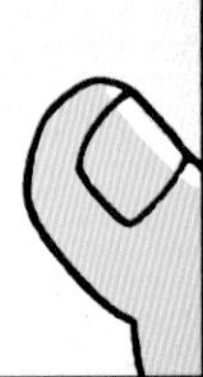

11:41

Sorry...

Are you a violist?

Yeah...?

So am I. Xin Liang.
Uh, hi! I'm Tate Seong.
It's nice to meet you. I've been looking for the rest of the viola section to introduce myself.
I am going to be first chair.

?

You should also work hard, so that the orchestra is the best it can be.

I'll try.

Please do. Have you met any other violists? There is still one who I can't find.
I've met one, I guess? Maya?
I talked to her earlier.
I guess you don't know the person I meant. I'm going to keep looking.
Um, bye?
Really cool...
We're going to miss you so much, kiddo! See you in a month!
tap tap
GROUP HUG

Work hard and have fun.
Dad, are you *crying?*

Well, it's clearly not sweat.
Hah!

YOU UP FOR THIS??
PROBABLY...

Goodbye, Tate!
Bye!
Don't forget to write us a letter at the halfway point!
I won't!

We love you!
I love you too!
...
11:52

YANK!

You're Eli Violet...
...aren't you?

II. DUET FOR 2 VIOLAS

WAH!

AH!

You've got the wrong guy! I'm not Eli Violet, I'm Eli...
...
Vance?
YEAH RIGHT.
All right, just listen. And close the door, I mean, jeez, dude.
I guess you got me. Yeah, I'm Eli Violet.

I dunno if you know this, but I was almost a pro viola soloist.
The thing is... at my breakout concert... I choked. I couldn't perform.
Ever since then, I can't play anything worthwhile in front of an audience.
But I'm not giving up.
I can't just waste all that time and effort I put into trying to go pro.
If I do things right, I can make a comeback.

So, I came to this camp, even when my parents kept saying I should take a break.
I'm not a quitter.
I'm gonna learn to be perfect again by the end-of-camp concert, and I'm gonna *get* that viola solo.
It's my first step back to being a pro.
clap!
clap!
clap!
...?
Oh! Sorry if I'm being weird! It's just...
...I'm kind of a fan?

Pssh. You're crazy, dude.

DUDE.
Well...my name's Tate! Nice to meet you.

Same.

One more thing: I'm here at camp anonymously.
The viola section's counselor is the only person who knows who I am...except you, I guess.
I wanna get that solo fair and square, without judges doing me favors because they know who I am.
So, is it cool if you keep all this a secret?
Totally cool!
Um...
You can say no to this. Like, no pressure, but...
Do you think you could give me some pointers on playing the viola every once in a while?

I'm not very good yet, but I really admire you, so I just thought...

Heh! Sure.

You made it sound like you were gonna say something weird, but that sounds fun.

Really?

Yeah, "really," doofus.

You and me are gonna be best bros.

BROS.

...

Welcome, all, to Camp Prodigy! "Where music is for everyone."
Our director would like to say a few words, and then you kids can head over to your cabins and get to know your sections.
Each cabin has a counselor who will be rooming with you, and they'll double as your instructor during sectionals.
If you have any questions or concerns, your counselor is your best go-to resource!
There won't be any activities or rehearsals today, so focus on settling in and looking over your music, all right? All right! Now, our director...

Hi, y'all! My name's Sunny, and I'll be your camp counselor for the month.
I play the viola too, so if you ever need help with your music, you can come to me!
Well, you can come to me for *any* reason—if you feel homesick, if you walked through poison oak, or if you just wanna talk! I'm excited to get to know you all!
So, first, how about an icebreaker? Introduce yourselves with your names...
...a fun fact...
...and, if you want to...
YOUR PRONOUNS.

huh?
what a pain...
haha
what?

Hi, I'm Tracy! I like cryptids, and I saw bigfoot in real life one time.
I guess I use she pronouns?
Tracy

My name is Aubrey, I use she/her pronouns, um...
I know how to use a sewing machine!
Aubrey

I'm Ivy. I use he/she pronouns, and my dad has a darkroom that I can develop photos in!
Ivy
If you want any camp pictures, give me your email!

I'm Eli. I like horror movies, and I use they/them pronouns.

Hi, my name's Tate!
One time I dunked a basketball at the park, like for real, and...
haha
hehe
My pronouns are...
...he/him.
...
This is the viola cabin!
We're right on the tree line, so we get the most shade.
CABIN ALTO
Nice, right?

Sounds like we've got the best chance at spotting a ghost!
Uh, nope. I don't mess with ghosts, dude.

hah
haha
Hey, aren't you the one who likes horror movies?
I like the **pool**– does that mean I gotta like the ***Mariana Trench***?

Go ahead and pick a bunk!

We've got storage under the beds for your luggage.

Tate, right?
Uh. Yes.
Have you picked a bunk yet?
Hahaha...
Well...Freddie's sitting all by herself over there.
How about you bunk with her?
Freddie?
UHHHHH...
Tate!
Wanna bunk with me?
PHEW
Sure!

Hey, Tate.

Wanna go practice?

Of course!

Yaaaaaaawn!

Maaaaan, I'm no good with so many people.
What? But you looked like you were having a lot of fun getting to know everyone.
I mean, yeah, they were cool and all, but I don't like having too much attention on me. You ever feel like that?
Haha... That's not really something that happens to me.
Anyway! Can we start working on this music?

Sure. How 'bout we start with some sight-reading?
Uh.
Sight-reading?
creeeeaaak.

C'mon, don't cry!
DOOM
No, it's just... I **told** you I was bad!
We all gotta start somewhere.
...
And the further back you are, the faster you can improve.
Just let me help, Tate. I think you could be really good.
You gotta relax your bow hand more.
Like this.
The old pancake wrist. You know better than that, right?
Your shoulder rest is at a weird height.
Let me.

All right, now try again. Your posture finally looks right.
Sure!
Wow, harsh.
sniff

It sounds better!
HI-5
Told you.
Now let's kick this piece's butt.
Hey, Eli?

SOLO
Mm?
Could you play through the songs too?
SOLO
I'm really bad right now.
SOLO
What? No way! Come on, please? Show me how it's supposed to sound!
Tate, I said I'm bad right now.

I guess you'd know better than me. I'm not a good judge of this stuff.

But that just means...

...no matter how many mistakes you make...
...it'll still sound beautiful to me.

Okay.
Okay?
Okaaaay. I'll play. Just don't make any weird faces at me.
You mean like you did to me?
hehe
Exactly!

THE
COMEBACK
QUICKSTEP!

Bravo!
Bravo!
APPLAUSE
Aw, shush. That wouldn't get me into any music conservatories.
Don't be humble!
I guess I never mentioned this, but you were the one who inspired me to learn the viola.
I don't think I could ever be disappointed in the way you play.
Uh, *what?* When'd you get inspired?
Technically, I've never had a solo concert.
I went to the one that you, uh, dropped out of.
I got kind of lost backstage before the concert, and I heard you practicing down the hallway.
It sounded so amazing... I just really wanted to be like that.

And I thought that, maybe, if I could play music like you, I could also be more... like me.
Tate?
It's a weird question, but...
You're not actually a boy, are you?
No, I'm not.

You're the first person I've ever told.
Awesome.
What pronouns do you use?
Oh, and should I be calling you by a different name?
T-they/them is good. And, yeah, Tate's still my name.

All right, Mx. Kindred Spirit! You wanna keep practicing or what?
EHEHEHE
Duh!
HEHEHE
HAHAHA
haha ha
hehehe
WEEK 1
DAY 2

That was a good first rehearsal, guys!
I'd like each section to focus on mastering a few specific things this week.
phew!

Cellists, you should get to work on the eighth note passage at section B
section F...
noticeable

...staccato...
...section H...

...section A...
...bring out the harmony...
...bow placement...
...third position...
WHAT DOES
THIS MEAN?
...violists...
...syncopated rhythms...
...section G...
...treble clef...

accelerando at the end.
Naturally.
And be very precise
dissonance
in the
da.
Yup, that's a no-brainer.

Well, that's it for today!
KO
Remember, there will be seating auditions this afternoon...

Chatter
chatter
Chatter
Who's ready for seating auditions?
chatter
Chatter
chatter
Chatter
Woo-hoo!
Chill out, you're way too excited!
I know, I know! It's just...at my school, I'm the only violist.
I'm finally going to be able to see how I measure up with other people!
Ohhh.
I'm actually nervous. Is that just me?
I wouldn't call it nerves. Maybe anticipation.
But that is not necessarily a bad thing.
You think so?
Whaaa? I don't think we have to take it so seriously!
You sound like you're talking about life or death!
chat
chat
DREAD...
...

LA/
LO
TING
TIONS
Ick...
CLAMMY...
WIPE
WIPE
Oh, great.
Banana?
Huh?
They calm the shakes! Potassium, I think.
Oh! Thank you...
No problemo!

You guys must be newbies!
Don't worry—auditions get easier the more you do 'em.
Thanks!
NOT A NEWBIE
Eli Vance?
It's your turn for the audition! Go on in.
grip...
Hey.
I know you're worried, but even if you make mistakes, I'm really excited to hear you play.

SEATING AUDITION RESULTS
2nd audition next week
1st violin
2nd violin
viola
cello
bass
chatter
chatter
chatter
chatter
nod

(7) Eli
(8) Freddie
(9) Tracy
(10) Aubrey
(11) Maya
(12) Tate
CABIN ALTO
Tate?
CABIN ALTO

Oh.
Hi.
Everyone's had at least one audition they weren't great at. You'll do better next time.

I always do this. If I get even a little bit uncomfortable, I clam up, and suddenly I can't do anything.
It happens when I try to talk to people, and when I try to be a good musician, and when I try to come out.
I'm such a wimp...
Hey, don't talk like that.
Listen, Tate.

I'm not doing this practice-together-every-once-in-a-while thing. That's silly.
I'll tutor you instead.
And when the end-of-camp concert finally rolls up, you'll be sitting at the front of the section, with me.
Really?
Yeah, "really."
If you help me, I'm sure I can be great! I'll aim for second chair...
And I'll go for the first chair solo.
We'll be the best!

Let's bet. If I make it to first stand, I'll tell every-one who I am.
And I'll play that solo perfectly and go back to doing everything I'm supposed to do.
If I make it to the first stand, I'll come out to my family.
Then there won't be anything to keep me from feeling confident anymore!
I swear on the $45 million Stradivarius viola.
Cross my heart!

III. VARIATIONS ON A THEME

WEEK 1 DAY 3

Good morning, campers!

Let's get to work!

Thanks for your hard work, everyone!
Go get some lunch.

Ah, that was fun!
Stretch
You don't feel bad about sitting so far back in the section?

Why would I? I'm just here to have fun!

Getting all competitive is kind of weird, right?

haha... right...

...

...

Should you really be thinking that way?

I do not think this camp is for people who are "just here to have fun."
There's no need to get overcompetitive, but you should at least try.
You don't want to hold the section back.
Hah, that guy is always so serious!

eh?
Xin! I've been in orchestras with him before.
He's kind of uptight, but he's nice.
And **wow** is he a good musician!
"NICE"?
Leah, hi!
...
Um...can I sit with you, Eli?
Yeah. No problemo.
Uhhhhhh... You seem kind of mad...

My stand partner is sooo frustrat-ing.
gaaaaagh!
I'm listening.

She's got no pencils, she n't flip the ge even hough she's ting on he inside, he keeps omping into...
tap tap...

And what's up with you?

Me?

Yeah. You seem like you're in a bad mood too.

Oh! No, I'm fine! Haha...

C'mon, I'm not just asking for no reason. I wanna be your friend, but it's tough when you never talk about how you feel.

It's... tough?

Yeah.

You said you always clam up, right? Try... unclamming for once.
Oh, um. Okay.

Okay!

First I had to muddle through the whole rehearsal, and then when it's finally done...

WEEK 1

DAY 6

SECTIONALS

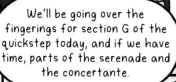

All right, y'all!

We'll be going over the fingerings for section G of the quickstep today, and if we have time, parts of the serenade and the concertante.

And if anyone wants to work on something else afterward, just ask!

Let's get started!
That's it for today. Good work, everyone!

haha
chat
chat
chat
chat
ssighhhhh
Aubrey.
GAH!
The syncopated rhythm at section C.
You aren't playing it correctly.
Oh...was it that obvious?
Yes. If you practice carefully with a metronome, you should improve.

You too, Maya.
Aw, shucks, ya got me!
And Tate...
You aren't doing too bad. Keep it up.
I've met plenty of people like him. Not a fan.
Really?
Yeah.
Competitive people just make playing viola more stressful.

But, hey, if things go the way we hope, you might end up sitting higher than him.
Wouldn't that be cool? The "weakest" violist beating the "best."
Might knock some sense into him.
The next seating audition is coming up, and...I've got a feeling you'll be moving up.
You bet I will!
WEEK 2
DAY 1
SEATING AUDITION RESULTS
1st violin
2nd violin
viola
cello
bass
Xin
(7) Freddie
(8) Eli
(9) Tate
(12) Maya

I...got ninth.
I got ninth chair!
SEATING AUD
NOOGIE!
8) Eli
9) Tate

WEEK 2
DAY 2
ACHOO!
C'mon, guys. Only half a mile left!
Okay!
KLIK!

You really like hiking, huh?
Yup! I like anything outdoorsy...
ACHOO
...but I guess it's not for everyone.
urgh
sniff
Is that her tenth or eleventh sneeze?
Hmm... Do I still have...?
Yes!
Hey, Freddie, here's a tissue. It's a little crumpled, but it's clean!
Thank you.
blow!
mumble
mumble

What are you reading? Don't you want to focus on the hike?
I gotta look over the audition sections from yesterday. See how I can improve.
Wait, what? You can do that later, right? Why not enjoy the-
Ugh, can you not distract me?
...
Hey, Tate.

Let's go practice.

Actually, let's not.
!!!

Wh-why?

It feels like something's up with you today. You've been acting kind of weird.

So...am I right?
glance...

Hey! You're the one who said no clamming up!
Aargh...

Okay, you're right. It's just... I...
I dropped a chair in the rankings yesterday.

WHAAAAAAT?! That's it?!
What the *heck?* Have some sympathy! I didn't come at you when you cried about sight-reading!
I DID NOT–
No, no, focus.
You're being too hard on yourself!
Eighth chair is better than me!
How about, instead of going to practice, we take a break?
Everyone's always saying that. I don't ***want*** to take a break.
...
10
10

You should listen to your friend.
If you push yourself too hard, you'll burn out. That'd just make for another setback.
?
YOU GAVE ME A TISSUE. I'LL LEND YOU SOME HELP.
That might be true, but-
Oh, come on!
We're at a summer camp! You should be having fun!
Here, I have a good idea for something fun to do.
How many peo ple have beer eavesdroppin on us?

Hup!
Let's braid lanyards!
YAAAAY!
Eh?
Good job!
Just remember that pattern.

Double helix.

Hahaha! What did you *do?* How'd it get that tangled?

Uuugghhh.

What's wrong?

Mine looks **horrible**.

It's all bumpy and weird. I'm terrible at this.

Hmm...

Yeah, you kind of are!

!

Well, yeah.
Of course I
know that.
Right?

Right.

10

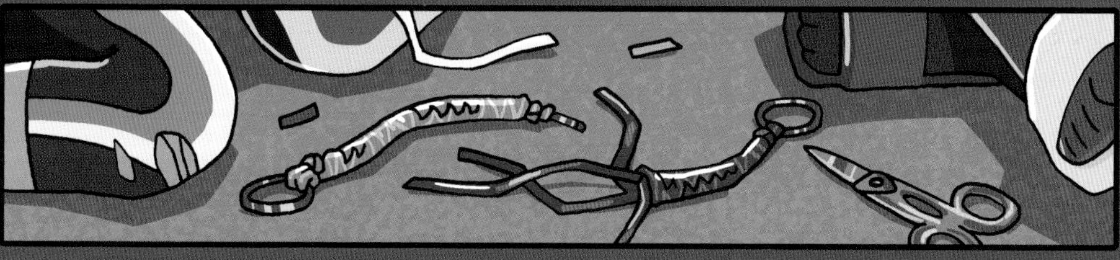

WEEK 2
DAY 3

DAY 4
Scaveng
Hunt

DAY 5
DAY 6

DAY 7
Hey, Eli?
Could you give me some tips on... coming out?
Are you gonna come out to Maya and Freddie?
Yeah, but...
Like I said, you're the only person I've ever told. I'm kind of nervous.
Sigh...

Makes sense.
How did you come out to your friends?
Streeetch
And, I guess, your family?
I mean, I've got two moms.
And some other queer relatives, too.
Being nonbinary isn't such a big deal.
But I guess I had friends who didn't get it, or who got awkward. So, here's my advice.
Oh.
You never really stop coming out.
When you meet new people, you've gotta decide whether or not to tell them.
It gets easier, sure, but it also gets more annoying. My only advice is...come out when you're ready.
Don't force yourself. This is your gift to them. They'd better appreciate it.

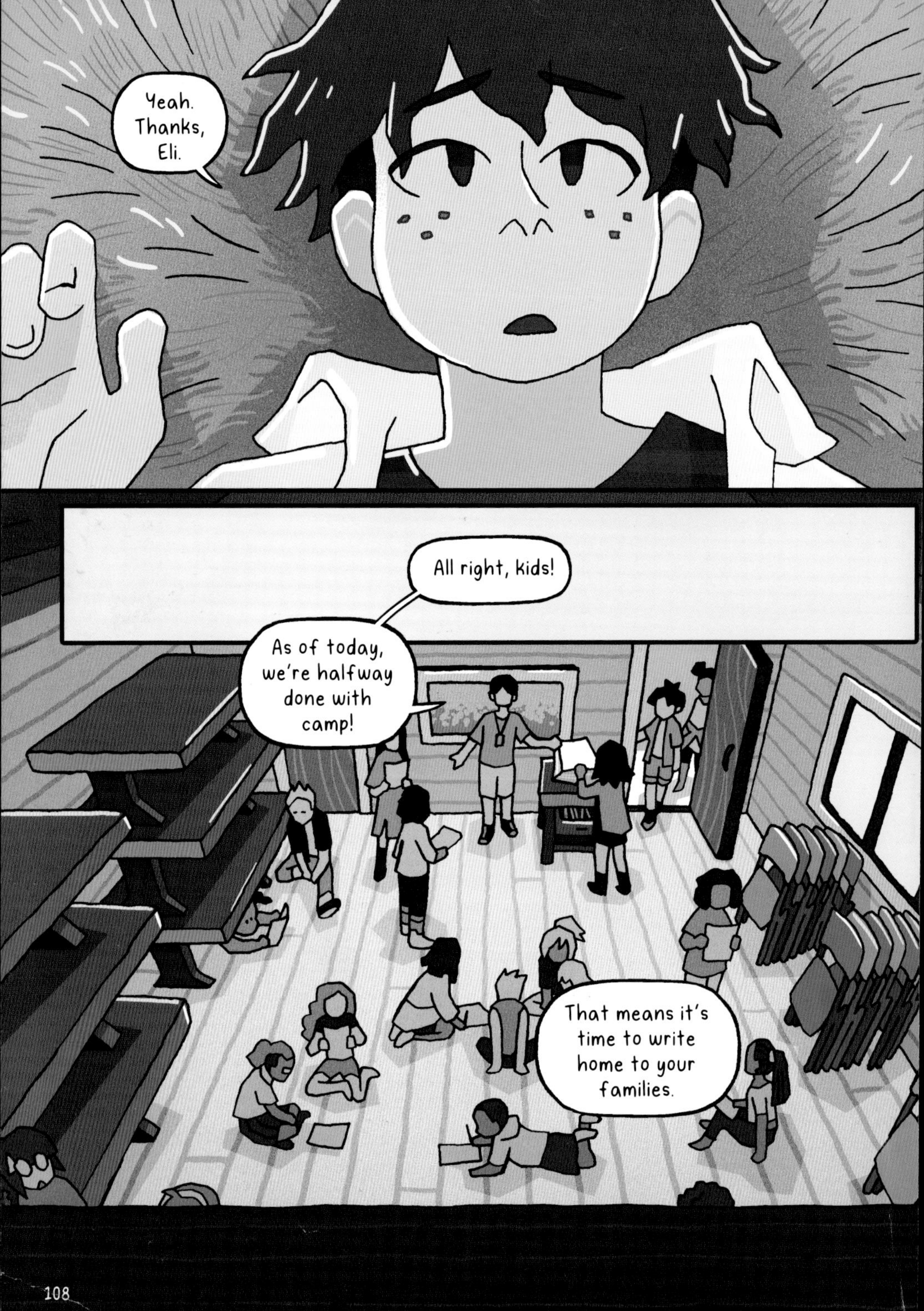
Yeah. Thanks, Eli.
All right, kids!
As of today, we're halfway done with camp!
That means it's time to write home to your families.

Please take one piece of paper and one pencil each.
If you need another, ask!
The letters are today?
Yeah, don't you remember? I'm gonna grab a spot; come find me!
There's so much to write about... How should I start?
I should definitely say I went from twelfth chair to ninth... And...
Oh, hey E-
Ah. Not Eli.
Where are they, anyway?

??

Just take deep breaths. Try to follow me, okay?

W-what's going on?
Eli, are you okay?
!
Tate, please head back to the dining hall. Eli needs some privacy right now–
It's... fine...
I don't... mind... if it's Tate...
Okay, but you can always change your mind.
What happened? Are you hurt?
How... do I tell them?
What?

How do I tell my parents I'm eighth chair?
What?
I know... they wouldn't be upset...
I know I shouldn't be worried, but...
I mean, they wanted me to take it easy...

I'm still...
scared.
It'll help you grow into a nice...
...young...
MAN...
Well, yeah, but the orchestra played something nice in the end. I just thought...
Eli Violet. She was weird, wasn't she?

You've really been improving since you joined the school orchestra.
I can't wait for your concert next week!
Of course!
If you want to.
It certainly came on fast. How did it start, Tate?
Eli Violet's concert!
Sit down, little bro. The doctor is *in*.
We're going to miss you so much, kiddo! See you in a month!
GROUP
HUG
we
love
you!

I know.

hah
heh
chat
haha
chat
crackle
crackle
crackle

WHOOSH!
Wah...
hehe

Here! You can have mine.
Oh, thanks!

here!

CHEERS!

SIIIIP

PWAH!

Everyone is being...extra nice to us right now.
Yeah, I noticed that!

Did something happen?
That's what we should be asking you!

EH?
Huh?

You both looked pretty down earlier.
We just want you to feel better!

UM!
I have something to say!

Yeah, Tate?

Um, so...
This isn't going to change our friendship! At all! Unless you, well...

So this is an important thing about me,
that I'm choosing to share with you,
You can do it!
?
?

Tate? What are you trying to say?
huff
huff

...

I'm nonbinary.

Ohhh! That's it?

HA HA

HA HA HA HA!

ha ha ha ha ha

haha

WEEK 3
DAY 1

You are suspicious, Tate Seong.

Could you be cheating?

Are you **kidding** me?! Why would I cheat? And **how** am I even cheating?

You've been moving up in the section very quickly. It's strange.
If you know the judges, or your parents funded the camp...or something...
What's your problem with me?!
Huh? Tate, I do not have any-
Yeah, *right!* Why else would you be accusing me like this?
I didn't cheat. I got this good on my own, by working hard.

...

Okay. Let's both just-
I think you're just **scared**.

Scared I might get better than you.
What?

Hey, Eli.

Do you want to go practice?
I mean... I was actually gonna...go tie-dyeing.

Oh! That's fine. I think I'm still gonna practice, but I hope you have fun!

No, I... I should probably go with you.
I mean, playing music is the point of the camp, and if I'm gonna get that solo...

No way! The point of the camp is having fun! It's summer!
Why do you want to play the viola solo so badly, anyway?
Well, because... I'm supposed to.
I mean, if I'm just gonna slack off all the time, why even play?
Because you enjoy it?
...
I really don't mind practicing alone!
I promise!
Go tie-dye! I'm sure it'll be fun!

chatter
stop!
hahaha
chatter
chatter
chatter
like this
Freddie? Maya?
Hmm?
Why'd you guys start playing viola?

Me first!
My aunt plays viola in an orchestra.
She used to let me strum her viola like a guitar, and I thought it was really fun...
...so I decided to learn how to play it the right way!
And the best part is meeting new people and making new friends.

My turn!
I read a web-novel about a violist and thought it was very interesting.
I wanted to learn how to play, and once I did, I realized I liked playing music, especially in an orchestra.
It's like a puzzle coming together. Very satisfying.

What about you, Eli?
It's been a long time, but at the beginning...I just thought it sounded pretty.

Well...what do you think now?

That's not really something I think much anymore.

Maybe it would sound pretty to you again if you focused less on technical skill and more on just enjoying the activity of making music itself?

Like...

...making bracelets.

Or tie-dyeing.

FLAP!

Snort!

Yeah.
Maybe.

Eli?

Can we talk?

So, uh...how d'you know my name?
Come on. Did you really think I wouldn't recognize you? Eli *Violet*.
Hah. Yeah.
You sure took your time asking me, though. Over two weeks.
Give me a break. You're all the way in the back of the section.
Like I could see you back there.

Hah... Yeah...

And more than that! I haven't seen you since you left Solaria Youth Orchestra to be a soloist.

Even though, uh... I guess that didn't quite work–
Hannah, dear, let us not talk about such delicate matters.
Right, sorry.

But... really...

What are you doing in eighth chair? You're the best violist in the section, by far.

Maybe that's not so important, actually.
At the beginning, I was aiming for first chair, to get that solo. But I've realized...
...I don't wanna do that anymore.

I really don't understand you, Eli Violet.

If *I'd* been that close to going pro, I'd never give up until I got it.

Well, dude, I guess we're just different.

WEEK 3
DAY 2
All right, everyone! Let's take a break.

Y'know, Tate...
Are you sure you wanna go for first stand?
Yeah! I'm totally sure! Now more than ever.
uwah!
Cool, cool, good for you... Um.
Sorry, I think I'm gonna back out of our bet, though.
I kinda like eighth chair.
Oh? I mean, that's fine! No pressure, right?

Yeah, yeah, no pressure.
But, then, what about pressure for you?
glance
Like I said, I'm raring to go! All I feel is confidence!
And if you aren't trying to get the solo, I think I actually have a shot of beating Xin to it.
It's like they say: pressure makes a diamond!
Or a bunch of broken rocks...
Um...are you still okay with tutoring me?
Pssh. Of course.
I'm in this with you for the long haul.

WEEK 3
DAY 4
...
Hey, guys?
Where's Tate again?

They're practicing.
They wanna be first chair.
Wooow!
We should wish them good luck the next time we see them.
Yeah! Though...
...I wish they would hang out with us more.
...

WEEK 3
DAY 6

Today is our last sectional before the concert.

We should use this time to fix everything we can.

And there are a lot of people who don't have section A down.

hehe!

Xin, it's impossible to play every single part perfectly. We've gone over our time, anyway.

In my opinion, I think ***all*** of you are ready for the concert!

I would define "ready" as having a good grip on every single part.
Well...
And I think several of us fall short of that. So-
Xin, quit it.
It's not fun for everyone when you talk down to them all the time.
CLAK
I'm not-
I'm trying to-
Okay, okay! Guys, calm down!
Though I think Tate has a point.
CLAP

Doing your best is important...
But so is having fun.
Now, let's pack up. Good work, y'all!
Hey, thanks for speaking up back there.

It can get tricky sometimes, corralling you kids. Haha!
CAMP PRODIGY
Hah, yeah!
A-and no problem!
I think you've really been breaking out of your shell, Tate.
It seems like you have a lot more confidence than you did at the beginning of camp!

YEAH!
I think so too!
Actually, I'm aiming for first chair now!
Wow, awesome!
I know! I'm gonna do my best!
Well, I'll be rooting for you.
I can't wait to hear you play!
CHE ERS
SODA!

WEEK 3 DAY 7

It's time for Camp Prodigy's Annual Trivia Night!

Partners will be randomly assigned— the team with the most points wins a prize— points will increase the harder a question is— kinda like Jeopardy!, babe-ay!!!

She's so excited.

Where did she get that hat?

I'll be selecting the teams!

Maya and Leah.

Hiiii!

Eli and Harper.

let me guess... aries.

I am not an aries.

Tate and Xin.

Campers, please take a seat at one of the tables.

HOW DID THIS HAPPEN?
All right! First question.
How much weight can an ant lift?
EW, BUGS!! Wait, but I know this!
Fifty times its own weight!
BZZZ!
Correct! Tate and Xin get five points. The next question is...

Bzzz!
1 PT
2 PT

BZZZZ
3 PT
10 PT

15 PT
25 PT
BZZZ

It's time for the final question!
This one will count for fifty points.
If you answer correctly, you could win it all!
yes! we can catch up!

How many points are there... on a standard Go board?
eh?
go?
SLAM
THREE HUNDRED AND SIXTY-ONE!!!
Congratulations! The winners are Freddie and Seb!

Oh, well. I did pretty good, anyway.

glance
This guy, though...

I guess **some** of us "fall short" of–
Oh, very mature!

If it bothers you so much, then why do you say stuff like that to other people?
I think that's the immature thing.

I only criticize others when I can back it up.
I would not tell them to do something I can't personally do.

Then don't get mad when I say you're bad at trivia.
But we aren't *here* for trivia. We are here to play music.

UGH.

Tate...maybe it does not seem like it, but the only thing I want is for our orchestra to be the best it can be.
I don't care if you believe me, but I wanted to say that to you.

Then I guess you won't mind if I win that solo tomorrow.

(1) Tate

SEATING AUDITION RESULTS

AUDITION RESULTS
1st violin
2nd violin
viola
cello
bass

The judges think that this is what's best.

Congratulations, Tate.

...Thanks.
That was weird.
Yeah...

Hello, *soloists!*

You've worked hard for this, and I'm excited to be rehearsing with you.

You can think of these private practices as something like sectionals!

Now, let's have a run-through!
They... They're really good!

And I'm...

That's all for today! Great work, everyone. I'll see you tomorrow!

THEY MUST'VE NOTICED.

IT WAS SO OBVIOUS.

THEY COULD TELL, RIGHT?

THEY COULD TOTALLY TELL I'M A
FA KE

Tate?
AH!!

You okay? You seem kinda distracted.

Oh! I guess I was just zoning out! Sorry, guys, hah!
You're fine!
chat
chat
...
haha
Okay, spill the beans.

Uh... what?

Don't play with me. You've been acting totally weird tonight.

Ah. Uh, you shouldn't hit that piano...
Tate Seong.
?
You told me you'd try to stop clamming up.
But what are you *right now?*
...
A clam.
Heh.
Exactly. So, get over here and tell me what's up already.

Well...
I'm starting to see just how out of my league I am with the other soloists.
It feels like I'm awful in comparison.
You're definitely *not* awful, Mx. Clam.
I mean...you can say that all you want. Doesn't mean I'll believe it...
Hmm...
Okay, here's my advice.
Distract yourself.
When you start to worry, force yourself to think about the pros, not the cons.
I dunno about this...
Like, for example...
DOUBT

You got your goal! Now you can come out to your family with confidence.
Right?
...
Tate...?
Right... Or, actually...
No. Playing a solo, catching up with the others, coming out... Why do I have to do so many things?
It's too much! I've had enough! It was so great to win this seat, but if it's going to be like this the whole time, I don't want it anymore!
I should've quit while I was ahead. I got too full of myself!
I thought this would be fun, but it's *terrible!*
Eli...

I don't want to be first chair. I'm done.

So that's it, right? I can be done now...
Right?

IV. FINALE
WEEK 4
DAY 3
Sounding great, guys!
We'll start rehearsing with the rest of the orchestra tomorrow, so take it easy tonight.

THERE ARE FOUR DAYS TILL THE CONCERT.
AND I HAVEN'T IMPROVED A BIT.

This isn't working.

Tate...
Is this how *you* felt?
Back at your solo concert?
How it felt...

LIKE ALL EYES WERE ON ME.
LIKE IF I MESSED UP, EVERYTHING WOULD BE RUINED.
LIKE I *HAD* TO PERFORM, OR ELSE.
I couldn't get up the nerve, though.

But...
...maybe it's different for me.
Maybe I *can* work up the nerve.
Maybe there's some trick to getting rid of stage fright.
Maybe muscle memory will kick in! Or I'll find the right motivation!
Because...
...even when you first played for me, and you said it sounded awful... I thought it was amazing!
Couldn't... couldn't I do that too?

That's not gonna happen.
Why not?
That's some cartoon stuff, Tate.
The truth is that there's no magical solution.
You can't dump your anxiety once you've "earned it."
That's not how real life works.
It's already hard to play a regular part when you've never stepped out on a stage.
How's it gonna be with a solo? What if you go out there in front of everyone and freeze?
What d'you think that's gonna do to your head?

I'll be honest with you. It sounds like you've got two choices.

Back out of the solo.

Or follow-through, knowing it might be the worst night of your life.

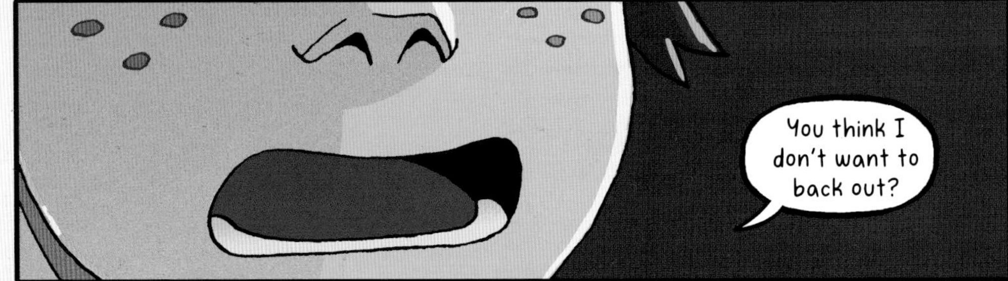
You think I don't want to back out?

Of course I want to! But I *can't!*
I'm the only violist who knows the solo! Who else has learned it?
Who else could play it right with such short notice, except for...?

Except for...

But that's not happening. I'm ***not*** going to make you take my place.

I'll do this myself. I'll deal with it, so...

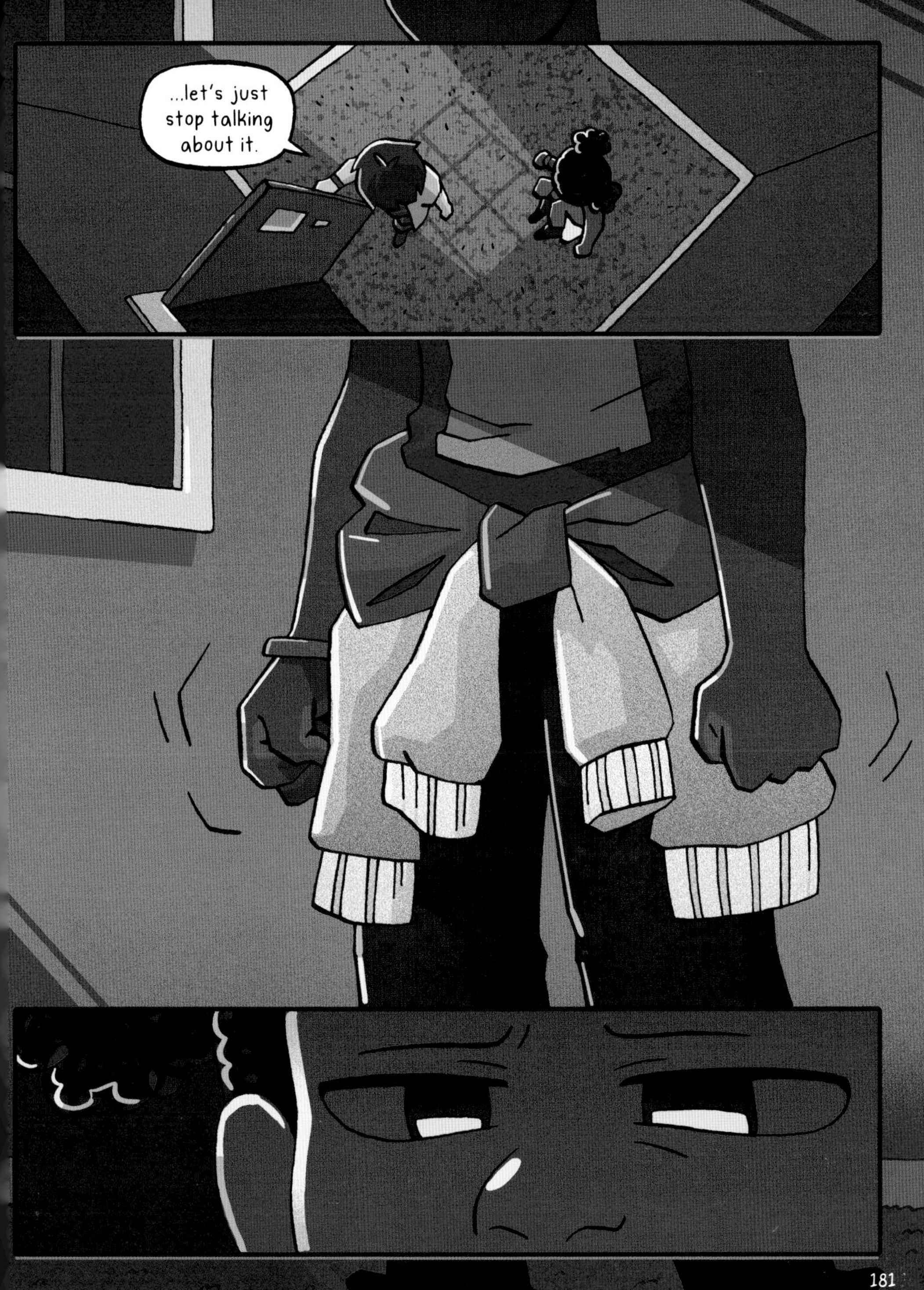
...let's just
stop talking
about it.

WEEK 4

DAY 6

Taaate...
Eliii...
Maya?
There you are!

Play some music with us!
Yeah, I don't think I can stomach looking at our sheet music right now.

What?
No, not that!

See?

Oh!

Talent de Lune (Main Theme)
The Regular Haunts Canon
Violin
You guys seem so nervous these days.
I thought it would be fun to do something low stress!
We're going to be like a viola-exclusive quartet, which is ridiculous.
I think it'll be fun to see how hard we can fail at reading the cello part, though.
So...what do you think?
Sounds fun!

hahaha!
hehe!

WEEK 4 DAY 7
Well. That's as good as it's going to get.
click
...

chatter
chat
chat
chat
chatter
chatter
chatter
chat

Hey, look!

Tate.

TAAATE!!!
Hi, kiddo!!!

We love you!! You're gonna do great!!

snort!

WAVE!
Does he look nervous to you?
It is his first concert.
...
Tate...
I know you said not to bring it up, but...

This really doesn't feel right.
...
I-
Viola section, group up!
We're having one last team meeting before the concert!
Gather round, y'all!
Shoot. Missed my chance.

It's almost time!
You guys have worked so hard this past month.
I'm very proud!
And I know you're gonna be awesome out there.
But if anyone's feeling nervous, or starting to get stage fright...
...you can always talk to me.
I'll do my best to help.

Wait.

Sunny, Tate's too scared to play the solo.
Wh-

What are you doing?
I can't just watch you do this to yourself.
Do you think I can just watch if it's *you*?

I'm the one who's played in a concert before.
I know this feeling, and...
...it won't be so bad for me. I can deal.
So, *I* should play the solo.

You asked me not to reveal you. I *promised*.

And I won't let you down in the final stretch.

Did you think I'd feel relieved about this?

Like, "oh, thanks for taking the pressure I put on myself and being miserable for me"?

I don't want that either!!
But *someone* has to play that solo!

I don't want you to get hurt!
And it's either *you*...or *me!*

Um.
Or me.

I've... I have been working on that solo since the beginning of camp.
SOLO
I thought that I would be first chair... And I really wanted to play it.

...Look.

This whole argument sounds very complicated, and I don't understand most of it.

But it sounds like neither of you want to play the solo. If so...

...I would be happy to take your place.

And if you have a problem with me...
I can play it too!
And me. We counselors try to be prepared.
I understand that you're under pressure.
But why are you trying to carry all of it on your own?
Look at how many people are willing to share the load.

Oh. Right. That's the whole point of opening up to people.
Friends...
Family...

The people who care about you...
When you're scared, or struggling...
...they'll want to help.
And you won't be alone.

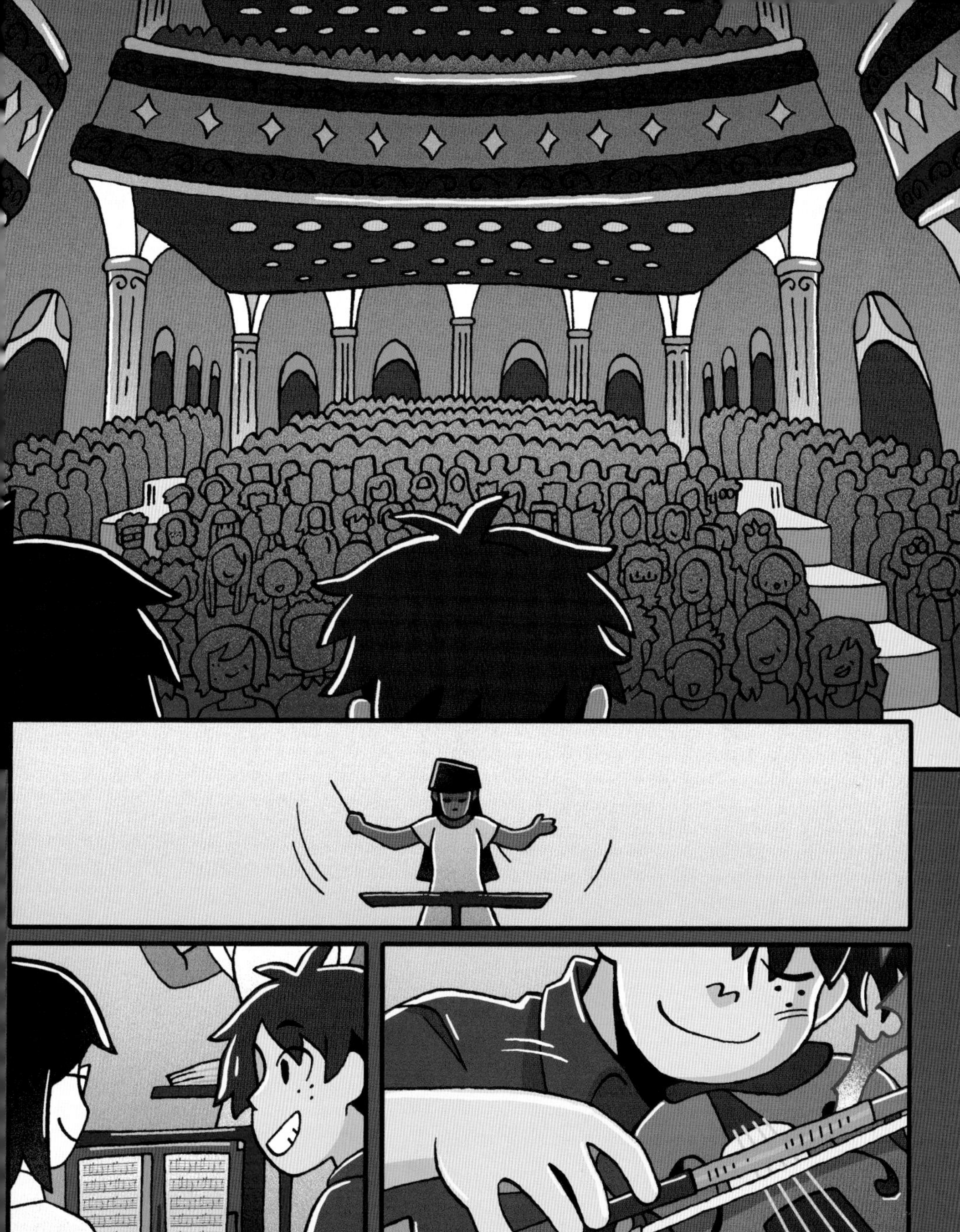

CLAP CLAP CLAP CLAP CLAP

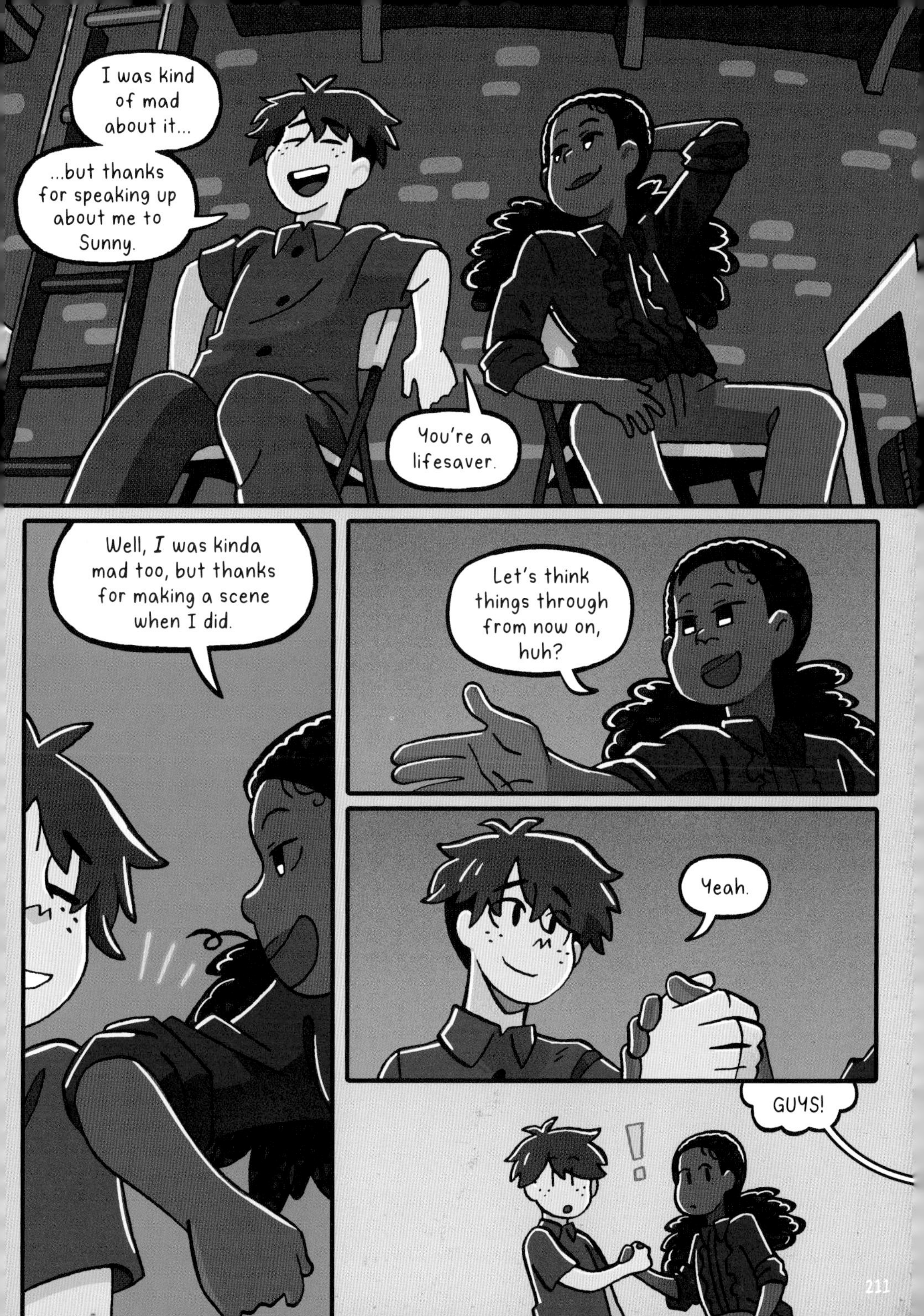

I was kind of mad about it...
...but thanks for speaking up about me to Sunny.
You're a lifesaver.

Well, *I* was kinda mad too, but thanks for making a scene when I did.

Let's think things through from now on, huh?

Yeah.
GUYS!
!

TACKLE!

Hi, Maya!
Great job out there!

Hey, Freddie.
What?

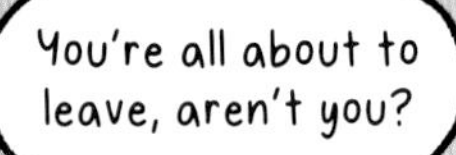
You're all about to leave, aren't you?
Could we, maybe... exchange phone numbers?
To keep in touch?

JOKER

Right?
I was thinking about that too.
What? Of course!

Yeah, I still need to pack up my viola.
I'm not ready to leave yet anyway, hah!
Well, I was worried!

Heck...
YEAH!
Friend group chat!
viola gc
hiiiiii!!
I've gotta go see my family, but I promise I'll keep in touch!
You'd better.
Ah, I'm so proud of you guys! You're gonna make me cry!
I didn't exactly reach my goal, though...

But you had fun, right?
Yeah.
I had more fun than I ever thought I'd have.
chat
chat
chat

Uh, hey, Xin!
Hello, Tate.

You played well out there.
Haha, thanks!

I, um, actually wanted to say something to you.

Thanks... and... sorry.

I told you I didn't cheat, but...
...in a way, I guess you could say I did.
For the past month, I've been tutored. By a really talented friend.

Being able to improve so quickly is still impressive.
You are a person I'd like to play beside again.
In the end, you got there without rigging the auditions or messing with the judges.
You did it with your own skill.

No matter how things turned out in the end, I don't think there is anything that should keep you from feeling confident.

Mom!
Mama!

You were a star out there!
We're so proud of you.

I...

And not just for playing well.

We're proud of you for respecting your own boundaries.

Instead of pushing yourself for achievements...
...you focused on your well-being.
We're so, so proud.
Of course I knew that!

inhale

exhale

Hey...

TAAATE

AH.

Oh, kiddo, you were *amazing!*

SQUEEEEEZE

Thanks, Mom–

How'd you get so good?

What sort of production are they running here?

Haha, you're so funny–Mom, I'm good.

How is she this *strong?*

You worked so hard...

He's already crying.

Um...can I say something?

I...actually wanted to say this after playing the first chair solo, but...

"I don't think there is anything that should keep you from feeling confident."

I don't want my confidence to depend on skill level. I've seen what happens when it does.

So...
squeeze
We're listening, kiddo.
hhh...

I'm nonbinary.
I'm not a boy...or a girl.
I'm...something different, but I'm still me.

I've thought about this... a lot.

I'm not just saying it on a whim.

Please trust me.

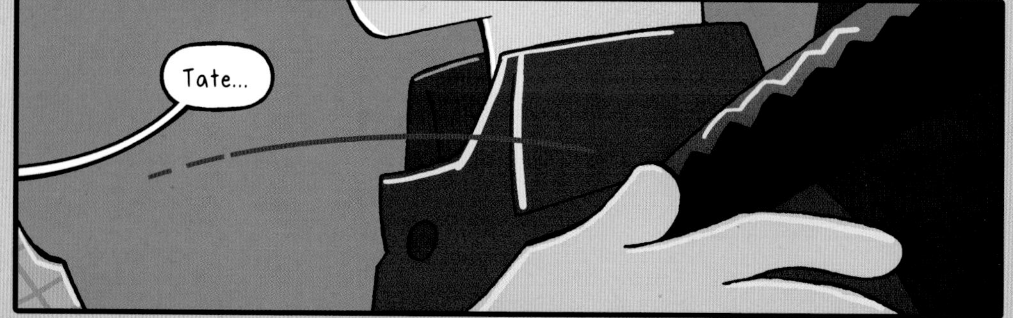

Of course we trust you.

You've always been a thoughtful kid. I know you wouldn't take...something like this...lightly.

I don't understand everything, but I can tell this is important to you. I'll do my best to learn!

We wouldn't ever judge you for this. You know that, right?
If anything we've said or done made you think we would, or made you feel scared to tell us...

...we're really sorry, Tate. We'll always love you no matter what.
Thank you for trusting us.

Heh.

TEARS.

Ack! D-did I say something bad?

Sniff...

(He's crying.)

No, no, I just– I...
hah

I'm *happy*.

FWUMP!
I love you guys too.

V. RHAPSODY

I heard you practicing upstairs. It sounds good, kiddo!
Thanks, Mom!
School's starting back up in a couple weeks! Are you going to take orchestra again?
Definitely! I want to show everyone how much I've improved!
Sitting out of any concerts this time?
No way!

pfft!

...if he can–
Oops! If they can
sign up for...

I'm going
to play a bit
more!
Have fun!

FWUMP
bzzt

!

Nat
thanks for always listening to me ToT
No prob! Actually, I wanted to tell you something important too
!! go ahead
m all ears!

tap tap
tap tap

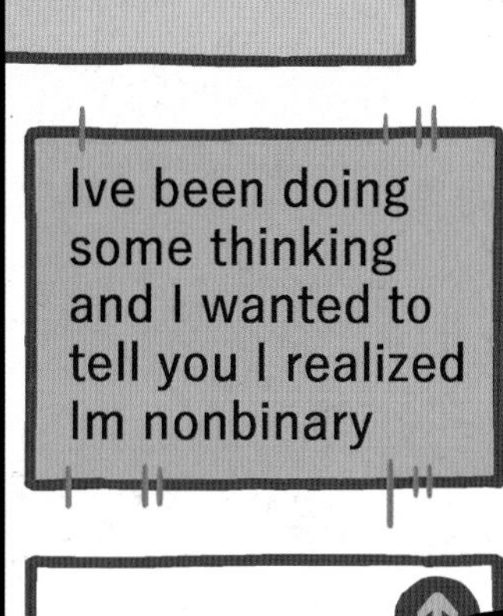

ank you for telling
ve heard a little
hat! do you use
ronouns then?

i'm really glad you felt like you could trust me with this. i used to think you didn't see me as a close friend because you didn't like to tell me about yourself, but lately we've been talking a lot more and i feel like i've really gotten to know you!
hank you again tate, i'm
eally honored TuT

Nat
Yea
tap
urse!!
Ive been trying to
open up
lately, its a
story
DING
Nat
open up
lately, its a
sto
I could tell you sometime :) Oh and yeah I use they/them pronouns!
Oh!
cicada quartet
lol
Lol.
DX DX DX
6:50 PM
ey just found some new music.you guys wanna play this next time we meet up?
Messages
cicada quar
hey just found
you guys wann
Nat
I could tell you sometime :) Oh and yeah I use they/them...
Xin
The Strawberry symphony is here for a tour, do you want...
Ian
Have you seen the new episode
If they sent more bug gifs, I'm gonna...
!

Definitely!
how about wednesday?
I can do that.
it's a date!! :D
wbu tate?

I wouldn't miss it for anything ^^

See you soon!

Acknowledgments

Throughout my life—and especially within these past two years—there have been so many people I've felt grateful for. Whether your name is written down here or not, I hope you know I appreciate you.

My heartfelt thanks to:

My parents, for supporting me so I could give *Camp Prodigy* my all, and for waiting patiently to read this book in its fully realized state.

My sisters, for letting me talk them to sleep for nearly eighteen years and for waiting not-so-patiently to read this book in its fully realized state.

My agent, Alexander Slater, for being an expert navigator through the world of publishing.

Alexandria Borbolla, for picking up *Camp Prodigy*. My editor, Julia McCarthy, for adopting it when it needed a new home, cheering me on, and making this book a breeze to work on. Karyn Lee, for elevating every bit of the design. Anum Shafqat, for being so organized.

The whole Atheneum team, for championing this book.

The people who taught me viola. Aram Bryan, for years of private lessons and encouragements to come out of my shell. Erica Hefner, for being a fantastic conductor and making orchestra a class I was always excited for.

Every fellow musician I've ever played with. There's nothing quite like the feeling of making music with your peers. My viola section—we held everything together.

Ngozi Ukazu, for mentoring me officially when I was in college and for mentoring me unofficially ever since. My fellow mentees and sequential arts majors, who are making their way in the world, I love all your comics. Every art teacher I've had over the years—there was never a boring lesson. Anne Trenning, for commissioning me as I found my way in the world of freelance art. It was always an exciting collaboration.

The friends who read my sketchbooks with fervor through middle and high school. I fell in love with comics, and you all were my biggest fans. The friends who shared my experience, being LGBTQ+—certainly an overlapping group. It was never quite so scary to come out when I knew the people who cared about me would accept me.

Grandma, for showing me early on that "Artist" was a possible career. My memories of making art together are always warm and sunny.

Concept Art

CAMP
PRODIGY

While drawing out this book, these were my go-to reference sheets. I used them to keep track of outfits, color palettes, and character body language. I'm not the sort of person who knows much about fashion or style, so I tried to push myself with these designs. For someone who wears a T-shirt and shorts on the daily, I think I did an okay job!

MAYA
casual
sporty
femme
excited
nervous
FREDDIE
excited
autistic swag
colorful
nervous
XIN
excited
mad
nerd
prep
summer
nervous
HANNAH
SUNNY
IAN
T-MOM
T-DAD

Development Sketches

This was some of the first art I did for *Camp Prodigy*. Some of the characters changed a lot as I figured out their personalities. Others didn't change very much at all.

The camp map is here as well! Though I originally drew it for myself, it turned out cute, so I sneakily placed it in a few of the pages of the book.

Xin

Sunny

FX CAMP

just a doodle

Eli's stand partner

skratch skratch

...

Maya

Hannah

More character explorations!

You tend to speak in a manner thats as unoffensive and benign as possible to everyone! ^^

Interests: viola, lanyards (past), reality TV, classical music, basketball (with friends at the park), multiplayer games (must be aesthetic/cute!), YouTube LetsPlays, chiptune game OSTs

you tend to speak in a manner that's laid back but kinda precocious at the same time

Interests: viola, punk fashion (just a bit), making little tunes/remixes in audacity, making stickers/charms/Shrinky Dinks/buttons, patching old clothes, any and all horror media

you tend to speak in a manner that's excited and cheerful!! :D sometimes you type to fast and make typos or grammer mistakes-

Interests: lanyards, broadway musicals, volleyball, swimming, anime (only the "normie" ones), baking (casually), gardening, roller skating, doing anything outdoorsy, bird-watching

You tend to speak in a manner that comes off as curt. It's not your intention to be rude, obviously.

Interests: playing cards/card games, visual novels, obscure webcomics/webnovels, hard sci-fi, writing (fanfic included), magic tricks, chess, Go, origami (complicated)

"You tend to speak in a manner that people call blunt or harsh but you think you are nice under it all."

Interests: obscure webcomics, viola, new media art experiments, drawing, obscure period-piece authors

Notable Dislikes: math, science, and history (bad at memorizing), slackers, vegetables, critics who can't do what they criticize

I wanted to figure out how everyone might talk and give them lots of minor interests, so they seemed more real. The background character designs are here as well; I had a lot of fun with those.

Save your critique of Ctrl+Alt+Del for when you can make something better!
......Do you consider that a difficult feat???
I mean... to be honest no.
the pretentious friends

"You speak in a manner that's peppy and encouraging!"

Interests: model ships and dioramas

"you speak in a straightforward and upfront manner."

Interests: cooking, writing

LEAH
hannah's nerd friend, 1st violin

TRACY
"big sis" of the cabin, viola

AUBREY
ultimate naive hypeman, viola

IVY
really excited!!!!, viola